THOMAS & FRIENDS™

Thomas' Read-Along Storybook

4 favorite stories with a read-along CD!

Based on The Railway Series by The Reverend W Awdry

Illustrated by Tommy Stubbs

Random House 🏠 New York

Thomas the Tank Engine & Friends™

A BRITT ALLCROFT PRODUCTION

Based on The Railway Series by The Reverend W Awdry.
Compilation copyright © 2007 Gullane (Thomas) LLC.

Thomas the Tank Engine & Friends and Thomas & Friends are trademarks of Gullane (Thomas) Limited.
Thomas the Tank Engine & Friends and Design are Reg. U.S. Pat. & Tm Off.

A HIT Entertainment Company

All rights reserved. Published in the United States by Random House Children's Books, a division of
Random House, Inc., New York, and in Canada by Random House of Canada Limited, Toronto. The stories in
this work were originally published separately by Random House Children's Books under the following titles:
Thomas Gets His Own Branch Line © 2002 Gullane (Thomas) LLC; *Thomas and Toby* © 2003 Gullane
(Thomas) LLC; *Thomas and the Castle* © 2004 Gullane (Thomas) LLC; *Thomas and the Magic Railroad*
© 2000 Gullane (Thomas) LLC.

RANDOM HOUSE and colophon are registered trademarks of Random House, Inc.

www.randomhouse.com/kids/thomas
www.thomasandfriends.com

Library of Congress Control Number: 2006938193
ISBN: 978-0-375-84182-8

PRINTED IN CHINA 10 9 8 7 6 5 4 3 2 1 First Edition

Contents

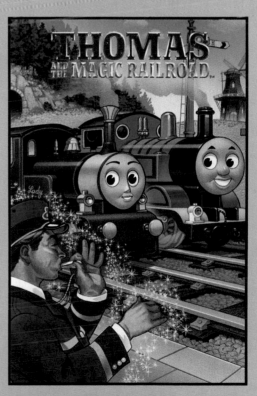

Thomas Gets His Own Branch Line

When Thomas first came to the Big Station, he was a cheeky little engine with no experience and not very many good manners. He liked to play tricks on the other engines. And sometimes he would rush to finish a job quickly and make a careless mistake. He thought that no engine worked as hard as he did.

Thomas had a lot to learn before he could become a Really Useful Engine.

One day, Thomas was shunting coaches in the yard. But he didn't think pushing coaches around was a very important job. He decided to play a trick on Gordon instead.

When Gordon came chugging into the yard, Thomas steamed out from behind a tree and overturned a truck full of cement right onto Gordon's wheels.

Gordon was stuck! "Now I cannot pull the Express!" he grumbled.

Thomas just laughed and laughed. *"Peep, peep! Peep!"*

But the joke did not seem *quite* so funny when Sir Topham Hatt came marching up with an angry look on his face.

"Thomas, where are the coaches?" he demanded. "People all over Sodor will be upset if the Express is late! Everyone expects this railway to be Really Reliable and Right on Time." Then Sir Topham Hatt hurried off to see if Henry could pull the Express.

"I'm sorry, Gordon," said Thomas. "I thought my trick would be funny." And he quickly went to get the coaches that he was supposed to have lined up earlier.

As he raced off, Thomas could hear Gordon still grumbling. "Cheeky little engine . . ."

Thomas worked quickly to get all the coaches. "Hurry, hurry," he pleaded. "The Express is going to be late!"

Thomas shunted all the coaches into place just as Henry was ready to go.

The Express was off, just in the nick of time!

When all the commotion was over and Gordon was unstuck and cleaned, Thomas got a good talking-to.

Sir Topham Hatt said, "Really Useful Engines do *not* play tricks when they have work to do! Shunting coaches may not seem important, but it is. If the coaches are not lined up properly, the passengers cannot ride the railway.

"*But* I am pleased that you worked hard to correct your mistake and get the Express going on time. Really Useful Engines take their duties seriously, and you have learned that every job is important."

After that, Thomas worked very hard. He played only *after* his work was done. But he wished that he could pull coaches filled with passengers instead of just pushing empty coaches around the yard.

One morning, Thomas' wish was granted. Henry was too sick to pull his morning route, and Thomas was the only engine left in the station.

"You'll have to pull Henry's train, Thomas," said Sir Topham Hatt. "We are counting on you. And *no* tricks!"

"Yes, sir!" Thomas hurried away. He just *knew* he could do as good a job as any of the big engines.

Thomas puffed eagerly into the station where the coaches and the passengers were waiting.

"Calm down, Thomas," said his driver. "Really Useful Engines are patient and careful with their work."

But Thomas didn't pay him any mind. He quickly backed up to the coaches.

Then, without waiting for the "all clear" signal, he chugged out of the station.

Thomas puffed along the line. He was very proud of himself. When he reached a "stop" signal, he slowed down in a huff. *Why should a speedy train like me have to wait for a pesky signal?* he thought. *"Peep, peep!"* he whistled impatiently.

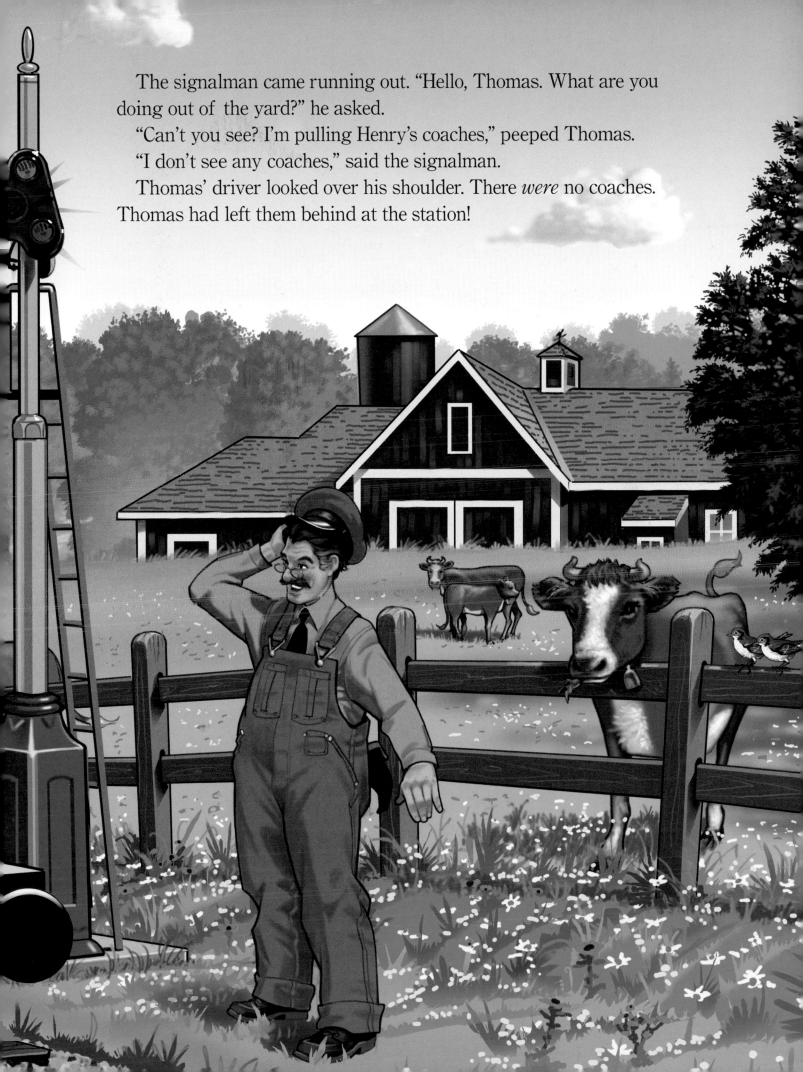

The signalman came running out. "Hello, Thomas. What are you doing out of the yard?" he asked.

"Can't you see? I'm pulling Henry's coaches," peeped Thomas.

"I don't see any coaches," said the signalman.

Thomas' driver looked over his shoulder. There *were* no coaches. Thomas had left them behind at the station!

Thomas was so disappointed that he almost cried.
"Don't worry, Thomas," said his driver. "We'll go back
and get the coaches straightaway."

Thomas went back and got the coaches. He waited until the coaches were properly hitched. Soon they were back on schedule. At each station, Thomas was very careful to let all the passengers on and off. "Thank you, Thomas," they said.

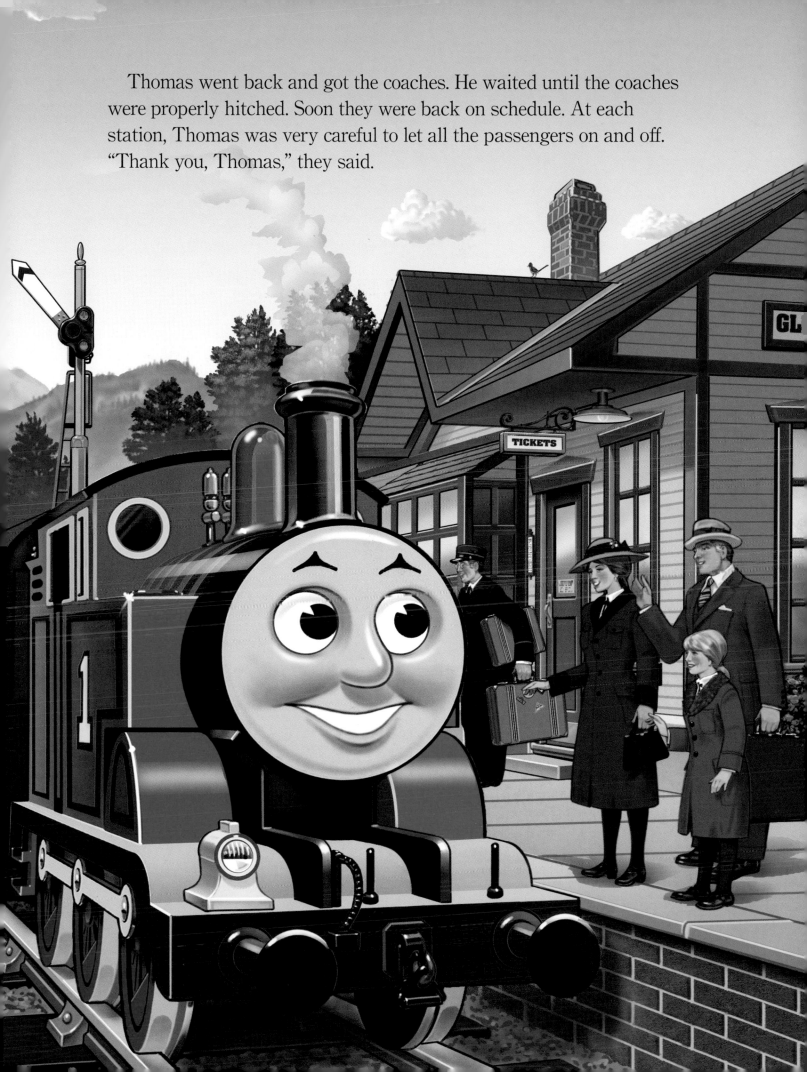

When Thomas got back to the yard that night, he was very tired. Pulling coaches was harder than he had thought. Sir Topham Hatt was waiting for him, trying not to smile.

"You did just fine, Thomas, once you remembered to get the coaches. . . ." Sir Topham Hatt chuckled. "More important, you learned something: Really Useful Engines are patient as well as speedy."

The next week, Thomas was pulling the afternoon train. When he came to the first station, he noticed an engine that wasn't on the track. "Hello, I'm Thomas," he said. "Why aren't you on the track?"

"Pleased to meet you, Thomas. I'm Bertie. I'm not on the track because I'm not a train. I'm a bus. Buses take passengers just like trains, but we drive on roads instead of on tracks," Bertie said.

"Well, a *bus* can't be as fast as a *train*," said Thomas cheekily. "I bet I can get to the end of the line before you." And he raced off.

Thomas was trying so hard to beat Bertie that he forgot to stop at the stations to let the passengers off! They started to get angry. Thomas' driver shouted, "Stop, Thomas, stop!"

But Thomas was going so fast that he could only hear the wind whistling.

Thomas got to the end of the line. "I won!" he peeped. "I *knew* trains were faster than buses."

"But, Thomas," the driver said angrily, "you haven't let any of your passengers off."

"Oh, no," gasped Thomas. "How will I get all these people home before dark?"

Just then, Bertie came driving up. "I'll help you," said Bertie.

"You will help me?" Thomas asked. "Even though I was very cheeky?!?"

"Of course," said Bertie. "We all help each other on the Island of Sodor."

And Thomas and Bertie split up the passengers and took them all home.

Once again, Thomas got a talking-to from Sir Topham Hatt. "Thomas, today you made two mistakes: one when you raced against Bertie and another when you forgot to let off your passengers. But in the end, you and Bertie got all the passengers safely home. I hope you have learned that although trains and buses are different, it does not mean that one is better than the other. *And* things work out when you work together."

Thomas *was* learning new lessons every day, and he really liked his new responsibilities. One day, he was pushing some Troublesome Trucks in the yard when he saw James going by much too fast.

"Help, help!" James called. "The trucks are pushing me too fast. And my brakes are on fire!"

The Troublesome Trucks only laughed and called, "On, on! Faster! Faster!"

Thomas acted quickly. He hitched
himself to the breakdown train and hurried
down the line after James.

When Thomas found James, he had run
right off the line and was lying in a muddy
ditch.

Thomas helped to get James and all the
trucks back onto the track.

"Thank you, Thomas," said James. "You
knew *just* what to do."

When Thomas and James got back to the yard, Sir Topham Hatt was waiting for them. "Thomas, I am very proud of you. You were brave, cool-headed, and helpful. You have grown quite a bit from the cheeky little engine you used to be. You have proven that you truly are a Really Useful Engine. Because you have done such a good job, I have decided that you shall have your own branch line!"

Thomas couldn't believe it. He was so excited. *"Peep, peep, peeeeeeeep!!"* he cried happily as he raced around the yard.

Now Thomas is proud of all the things he learned. He has two faithful coaches of his own. They are named Annie and Clarabel, and he loves pulling them up and down his very own branch line. Thomas always knew he would become a Really Useful Engine.

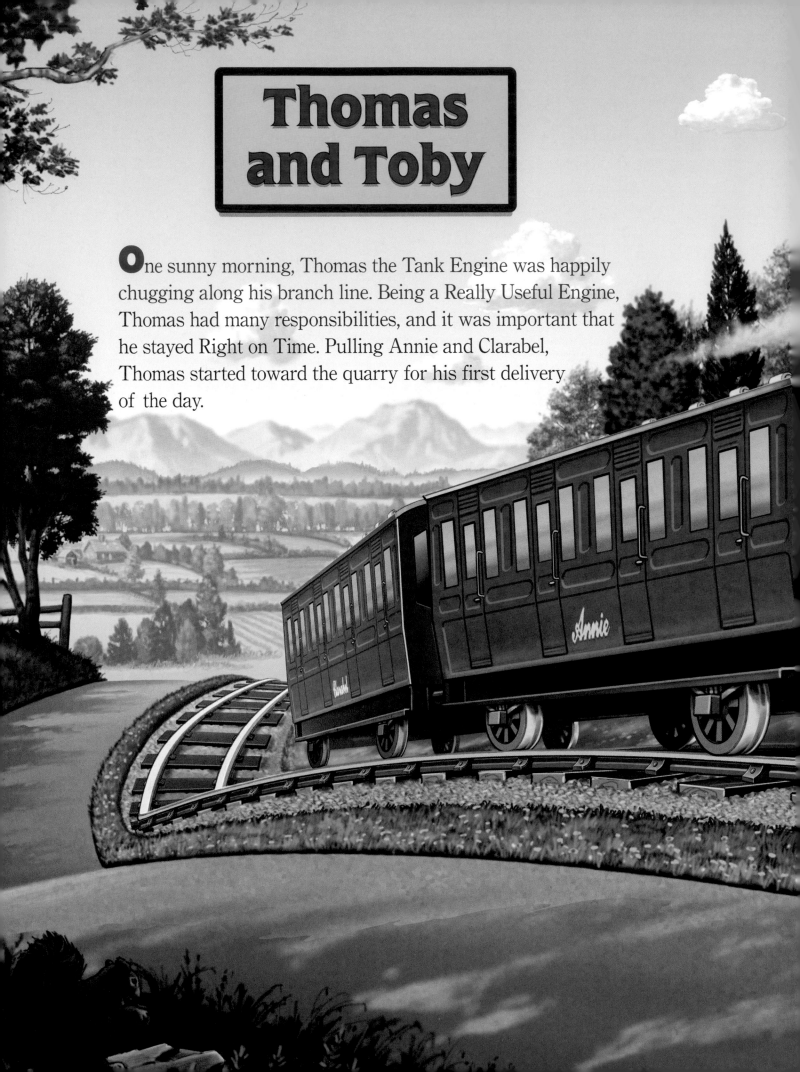

Thomas and Toby

One sunny morning, Thomas the Tank Engine was happily chugging along his branch line. Being a Really Useful Engine, Thomas had many responsibilities, and it was important that he stayed Right on Time. Pulling Annie and Clarabel, Thomas started toward the quarry for his first delivery of the day.

Thomas was especially careful on one part of his branch
line because it ran beside a long stretch of road.

"*Peep, peep!*" He'd whistle hello to anyone who might be
near, so they'd have plenty of time to get out of the way.

This late summer morning, as Thomas chugged around a bend, he noticed a policeman standing by the next crossing. Thomas had been close friends with the old constable, who'd recently retired.

This must be the new constable, thought Thomas, and he greeted the policeman with a friendly *"peep, peep."*

But the new constable's reply was far from friendly.
Thomas had startled him, and he stopped Thomas in his tracks.
"My very first day, and already there's trouble. Just who
are you and where do you think you are going?" asked the
red-faced policeman.

Thomas did his best to explain, but the policeman was not in a mood to listen to an engine.

"No cowcatcher? Not a single side plate in sight? You shouldn't travel near these public roads. It's too dangerous!" he exclaimed as he inspected Thomas.

"This cannot continue. I must speak with the person in charge."

Thomas told him that Sir Topham Hatt, the head of the railway, was on vacation. There was nothing Thomas could say to calm the policeman and nothing to do until Sir Topham Hatt returned.

"Troublemaker," muttered the policeman as Thomas chugged sadly away.

Sir Topham Hatt was having a much better time than Thomas.
He was vacationing with his family on the other side of Sodor. His
grandchildren had discovered an old-fashioned steam tram that still
gave rides to passengers.

The short and sturdy tram's name was Toby. He had cowcatchers,
side plates, and a cheery bell that he rang to greet all he met. He
traveled with Henrietta, a tram coach whom he considered a good, if
sometimes fussy, friend.

Long ago, they were very busy transporting goods and people to
the Main Line. But now almost everyone traveled by cars and buses.
Toby and Henrietta spent their days giving tram rides to people on
vacation.

Being the kind of family who enjoyed railways, the Hatts returned to Toby every day of their vacation for a ride. It didn't take long for Toby to recognize that Sir Topham Hatt was a special passenger. He asked all the right questions and knew just about everything there was to know about trains and trams.

"What is your name?" asked Sir Topham Hatt as the Hatts took the last tram ride of their vacation.

"Toby, sir."

"Thank you, Toby, for a very memorable vacation."

"Thank you, sir," said Toby politely. Toby thought to himself, *This gentleman is a gentleman who knows how to speak to engines.*

Sadly, a few days later, Toby and Henrietta's line was shut down and they were sent to their sheds.

When Sir Topham Hatt returned from vacation, he was informed immediately about Thomas' trouble with the new constable.

He remembered Toby. He knew that underneath the chipped paint and rusty spots was a very useful tram engine who could handle the quarry line . . . *and* the prickly policeman. And there were plenty of other things to keep Thomas occupied as well.

Soon Toby and Henrietta arrived and they took to their new jobs very quickly. Toby was especially good at making the trucks behave. Thomas noticed this right away and was very impressed. He knew firsthand how troublesome those trucks could be. In no time, Thomas and Toby became good friends.

James, however, was not at all impressed with Toby. He often met Toby and Henrietta at the junction. Every time he saw them, he made a crack about how dirty they were or how slow they moved.

One day, Toby had had enough. "*Whoosh*," Toby cried, blowing out a great burst of steam. "Why must you always be so mean?"

"Oh bother," replied James. "I don't have time right now for dirty, slow engines like you. Really splendid, fast engines like myself have lots to do." Off he sped to his next stop, leaving Toby in a cloud of steam.

James continued on his route, picking up more and more trucks. He was still a bit cranky and very distracted. As he was traveling down Gordon's Hill, James was so busy thinking of things to say to Toby that he forgot to pin down his brakes. Faster, faster he flew as the trucks bumped and pushed him down the steep hill, for they loved to go fast and make trouble.

"I've got to stop," screeched James as he pulled on the brakes.

But it was no use. James could not slow down.

"Hurray," cheered the trucks . . . and then . . .

Crash!

James had finally stopped at the bottom of the hill. He'd run straight into two tar wagons.

What a sticky, dirty mess!

A short time later, the breakdown train and all available engines arrived to help with the cleanup. Toby immediately started getting the trucks under control.

When he saw James, Toby couldn't resist having a little fun.

"Is that *James*?" Toby asked innocently. "It can't be. James is such a splendid, fast engine."

James pretended he didn't hear Toby. And from that day on, James was a lot nicer.

Toby knew just about everything when it came to moving trucks. He had many years of experience and a very patient nature. So Sir Topham Hatt asked Toby to coach Mavis, a new diesel engine at the Ffarquhar Quarry.

Like most new engines, especially diesels, Mavis thought she knew it all, or at least more than that old-fashioned tram did! She quickly grew bored with moving the trucks at the quarry. More than anything, she wanted to be on the line.

One wet but very busy day, Toby asked Mavis to bring the trucks
to the line. Mavis was thrilled.

"Take it slow," he warned.

"Watch the wet rails," he suggested.

"Keep an eye on the trucks," he reminded.

But Mavis was too excited to pay attention to Toby.

As soon as she started on her way, though, she wished she'd listened more closely. The trucks realized she was new at this. The cold autumn rain made the rails extra slick, so they bumped and pushed, and before she knew it, Mavis was stalled right in the middle of a busy crossing.

Soon there were many angry people who needed to get by. Mavis didn't know what to do, and the trucks just laughed at her. She knew that Toby would be angry.

And he was. But Toby also remembered that it was Mavis' first time on the line and how tricky those trucks could be. He helped Mavis out of the crossing and promised to spend more time teaching her at the quarry.

Toby had been there only a short while, but already his hard work was recognized. Sir Topham Hatt gave both him and Henrietta a long-overdue fresh coat of paint and some shiny new parts. And best of all, Toby got a new number of his own. Now he, too, truly was a Really Useful Engine.

Toby and Thomas' friendship grew and grew. Thomas especially liked it when he found out that Toby always startled the not-so-cheery policeman with a cheery ring of his bell!

Thomas
and the Castle

It was a fine fall morning on the Island of Sodor, and Thomas was looking forward to pulling coaches on his branch line. But Percy was telling ghost stories. "My driver saw the *ghost train* last night. They say that it appears to engines once in a while as a warning of trouble ahead."

"Pooh," said Thomas. "Silly Percy! Really Useful Engines don't have time for ghost stories. *I'm* not scared."

The next evening, Percy was coming home from the harbor. He was humming along the rails, almost to Crowe's Farm Crossing.

Little did Percy know that a cart of flour was stuck
on the tracks at the crossing!

Percy came upon the cart swiftly in the dark. He smashed it to smithereens in a billowing cloud of white flour!

When the dust cleared, Percy was a ghostly white. "Whew," said his driver. "I'm glad no one was hurt, Percy. But you look like a ghost. Let's go get you a washdown."

"Let me stay this way," said Percy. "I think I know someone who deserves a good scare!"

On the way home, Percy came upon Toby and convinced him to help scare Thomas. Toby pulled into the yard first and told Thomas, "Percy's had an accident!" Just then, ghostly Percy rolled up, making an awful moaning and clanking sound. Thomas was so scared, he hurried out of the yard.

Percy and Toby had a good laugh. "That will teach Thomas to say I'm a silly engine," said Percy with a smile.

Thomas soon figured out that Percy was only fooling about being a ghost. And a couple of days later, when James came home with another scary story, Thomas thought the other engines were still playing tricks on him.

"I saw spooky lights floating around Rolf's Castle tonight," said James.

"But that castle has been abandoned for years," said Gordon.

"Maybe it's a ghost," guessed Percy.

"Pish posh," said Thomas. "You won't fool me again."

A week went by, and Thomas forgot about silly ghost stories . . . until he met Bill and Ben at the crossing one morning.

"Thomas, you won't believe what we saw last night!" said Bill.

"There were ghosts inside Rolf's Castle," said Ben.

"Spooky," said Bill.

"Creepy," said Ben.

"And then," said Bill, "the signal was green when it should have been red. I almost crashed into Ben."

"Spooky," said Ben.

"Creepy," said Bill.

Thomas thought that Bill and Ben were probably just teasing, but he was still uneasy. He asked Sir Topham Hatt for routes that would take him far from Rolf's Castle. As he was getting ready to take some Troublesome Trucks to the mine, Gordon came chugging up.

"Thomas, why are you going to the mine?" asked Gordon. "Are you afraid of Rolf's Castle?"

"I'm not afraid of anything," wheeshed Thomas. And he chuffed away.

"I'll show him," said Thomas.
"Scaredy-cat. Scaredy-cat,"
sang the trucks.

Thomas didn't know it, but the mines were a dangerous place. Long ago, miners had made tunnels, and some of their roofs were not strong enough to hold up an engine, even one as small as Thomas. There were danger signs everywhere.

But Thomas was still stung by Gordon's and the trucks' taunts. *I'm not afraid of a silly old sign,* thought Thomas.

To prove he wasn't afraid, Thomas bumped some empty trucks fiercely, sending them right through a sign and onto the siding beyond. Thomas foolishly followed the trucks right onto the dangerous siding. "Hurrah," laughed Thomas. "There's nothing to be scared of!"

Just then, the rails started to quiver. The track gave way,
and Thomas sank into the mine!

Gordon had to be sent to pull Thomas out of the hole. "Thanks, Gordon," said Thomas. "I was just trying to prove I wasn't scared of anything."

"That's okay," said Gordon. "I'm sorry I made fun of you."

Thomas decided that being foolish was not the same as being
brave. So when Sir Topham Hatt needed an engine to pull a Special
right to Rolf's Castle, Thomas volunteered. He wanted to be a Really
Useful Engine.

As Thomas started off for the castle, night was falling and fog was rolling in. Thomas was very afraid, but he chugged on bravely. Ahead in the fog, he saw an eerie glow. *It's a ghost!* he thought. *Just like the one James saw.*

But as Thomas came up the hill, a brisk wind blew and the fog cleared. Thomas saw that there was no ghost at all. It was just the fog man with his lantern. Thomas realized that James hadn't seen a ghost after all. Just lanterns in the fog. But what were lanterns doing in an abandoned castle?

Although the fog had blown away, the moon was still behind the clouds. When Thomas saw something white fluttering up ahead, he was *sure* it was the ghost this time! "Don't be scared, don't be scared," he huffed to himself.

Thomas chugged bravely on and realized that the fluttering white thing was . . . *curtains! Well, bust my boiler,* Thomas thought. *Maybe the ghosts Bill and Ben saw were just curtains. What is going on here?* It was all a mystery.

When Thomas approached the signal near the castle, it was flashing red, then green, then red again. "That's funny," said Thomas to the signalman. "Bill and Ben were having problems with this same signal the other night."

But Thomas wasn't scared anymore. He thought he might have an idea what was going on at the castle. He asked the signalman, "Are there people moving into the castle?"

"No, but your guess is close," said the signalman. "They are restoring the castle. And the electrical work they are doing has been causing my signal to go haywire. But, Thomas, you'd better move on . . . they're expecting that load you're pulling."

When Thomas finally arrived at Rolf's Castle, Sir Topham Hatt was there, getting ready for a big party to celebrate the reopening of the castle!

Thomas was relieved that there was nothing to be scared of after all. He was also proud to have figured out the mystery. "Thomas," said Sir Topham Hatt, "you have been brave and clever. You are a Really Useful Engine."

Thomas and the
Magic Railroad

Thomas the Tank Engine is a little blue engine who lives on the Island of Sodor. He has many engine friends, and they all try to be Really Useful.

There was harmony on the Island of Sodor until, one day, a mean diesel engine arrived. He was called Diesel 10, and he hated steam engines.

"Get out of my way, you puffballs!" he growled as he sped past Thomas and Gordon the Express Engine. "When I'm done with my plan, you'll be nothing but useless scrap!"

Thomas was scared of Diesel 10, but he knew he had to be a brave little engine.

Far away from the Island of Sodor, across a wide ocean and on the other side of Muffle Mountain, was the town of Shining Time. It was the home of Mr. Conductor, who comes and goes in gold dust.

Mr. Conductor was getting ready for a trip to the Island of Sodor on the Magic Railroad. The Magic Railroad was a Conductor Family Secret.

The engines were very glad to see their friend Mr. Conductor. He would take care of them while Sir Topham Hatt, the railroad director, went on vacation.

But Diesel 10 had other plans.

"I'll soon settle Twinkle-Toes with my claw," he snarled.

That night, Diesel 10 sidled up to the shed while Mr. Conductor and the engines were asleep.

"Gold dust . . . magic . . . buffers," Mr. Conductor mumbled in his dreams. He woke up remembering what his family had always told him: *As long as there is gold dust, there will be harmony.* He blew his whistle, but it had no sparkle.

"Oh, no," cried Mr. Conductor. "I've got to find more gold dust to run the railroad or we will all be in danger!"

Diesel 10 slunk quietly away.

Using a bellflower, Mr. Conductor called his cousin Junior and told him to fetch the emergency supply of gold dust from Shining Time Station.

About that time, a young girl named Lily arrived at Shining Time, led by a friendly dog called Mutt. Lily had come from the Big City to visit her grandpa, Burnett Stone, who lived on Muffle Mountain.

The trains didn't stop on Burnett's side of the mountain, but that night Lily heard the sound of a train whistle outside her window.

The next morning, Thomas went to fetch coal for Henry, who had boiler ache. The last freight car wasn't coupled properly to the others. It glided through an old set of buffers and disappeared.

Meanwhile, a very tired Mr. Conductor was searching for the source of the gold dust. Diesel 10 caught him walking along a viaduct. Diesel 10 grabbed Mr. Conductor with his claw and dangled him over the gorge! Mr. Conductor yanked out his pliers and cut one of the cables connected to Diesel 10's claw.

The claw sprang open and flung Mr. Conductor onto a sack of grain at the base of a windmill. There he found a clue to the source of the gold dust. It said: *Stoke up the magic in the mountain, and the Lady will smile. Then watch the swirls that spin so well.*

Back at Shining Time Station, Lily met Mr. Conductor's cousin Junior. He appeared in a wonderful cascade of sparkles. Junior was on his way to the Island of Sodor. He asked Lily to go with him.

"I'll use the last of my cousin's gold dust," said Junior. "It's the only way to travel, and we'll find lots more soon."

Whoosh! Suddenly, they were on the Magic Railroad, moving bumpily along. The gold dust made little pools of light in the dark tunnel.

The two of them glided right through the buffers at the end of the track. Lily's eyes widened when she saw the Island of Sodor in all its marvelous magic.

"I was at the old buffers when the last coal car disappeared," Thomas was saying to Percy.

"Then I think those buffers are the entrance to Mr. Conductor's Magic Railroad!" Percy said excitedly.

"Percy, you are clever!" said Thomas. "Now keep the buffers safe while I search for Mr. Conductor."

To Thomas' surprise, he found Junior instead! Junior introduced Thomas to the astonished Lily. She couldn't believe that trains could talk! In no time at all, Thomas was puffing along with Lily and Junior on board. Junior spotted his cousin at the bottom of the windmill.

"Howdy, cuz," Junior said.

Mr. Conductor smiled and gave his cousin a hug.

In his darkened workshop, Burnett Stone was working on the beautiful golden steam engine called Lady. It was Lady's whistle that Lily had heard that night.

When Burnett was young, Lady was hurt in a terrible accident. Lady's beautiful face had faded, and the Magic Railroad faded with it. As hard as he tried, Burnett couldn't make Lady come back to life.

"The railroad needs Lady," whispered Burnett as he worked. "I need to know the secret to make her run again."

On the Island of Sodor, Diesel 10 was plotting to destroy the Magic Railroad.

"We don't know which buffers are the entrance to the Magic Railroad," he told his hench-diesels, Splatter and Dodge. "We'll just have to destroy them all!"

Percy overheard the diesels' plan and knew the engines had to act quickly.

"We must get Lily back to Muffle Mountain before the diesels destroy the Magic Railroad," Percy said.

"Without gold dust, the only way to travel the Magic Railroad is on the lost engine, Lady," said Mr. Conductor. "Unless . . . Thomas, you're a Really Useful Engine. You can do it."

"I'll try," Thomas said bravely.

As Thomas and Lily chugged toward the magic buffers, Mr. Conductor called after them, *"Stoke up the magic in the mountain, and the Lady will smile."*

They reached the buffers—and went right through them, onto the Magic Railroad! They spotted the missing coal car and quickly coupled it to Thomas.

Looming up ahead was a huge set of buffers. Thomas and Lily passed right through them onto Muffle Mountain! Lily jumped off Thomas and ran to Burnett's workshop.

Elsewhere on Muffle Mountain, a huge explosion jolted Thomas off the ground and onto another branch of the Magic Railroad. In this unfamiliar place, Thomas wasn't sure he could find his way back to where he'd left Lily. He hurried off to find a connection back to the Main Line.

At the same time, Lily rushed into Burnett's workshop, where she saw the beautiful golden engine. "This is the lost engine from long ago!" exclaimed Lily. "She's the key to Mr. Conductor's Magic Railroad."

"I don't know how to make Lady run," said Burnett sadly. But Lily suddenly realized that *she* did.

"She needs coal from the Island of Sodor!" Lily said. "Thomas and I brought some with us."

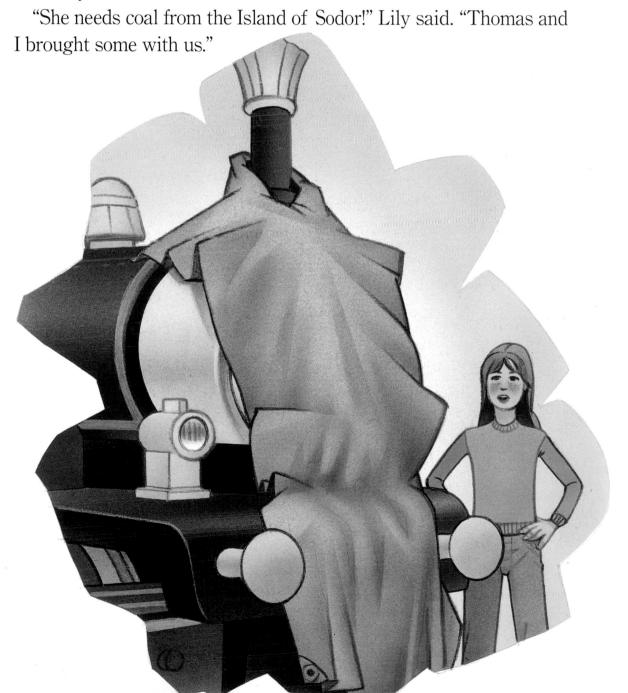

Soon, Lady was steaming along the Magic Railroad. As she gathered speed, her lovely face was revealed once again.

"Stoke up the magic in the mountain, and the Lady will smile," Lily murmured to herself.

The railroad's energy was returning. Shavings all the colors of the rainbow fell behind Lady and gathered on the ground.

Lily caught some shavings in her backpack. Then she saw Thomas about to meet up with the Magic Railroad's Main Line. As the shimmering shavings settled on the rusty tracks, Thomas gained traction and gathered speed.

With a long, low roar, Lady burst through the buffers onto the Island of Sodor!

Burnett, Lily, and Mutt jumped off Lady to join the others. Then Thomas burst through the buffers right behind Lady.

Suddenly, Diesel 10 appeared, as if from nowhere. With a roar, he rushed at Thomas, his jagged claw snapping.

"I'll get you, puffball," yelled Diesel 10. "And I'll get that magic engine, too!"

"Run, Lady, quickly—I'll help you!" called Thomas.

Burnett leaped into Lady's cab, and they sped toward an old viaduct.

Thomas raced between Lady and Diesel 10. As Lady crossed the viaduct, it began to crumble, and a hole opened in the track ahead of Thomas. Thomas bravely jumped the gap! But as Diesel 10 closed in, the rest of the viaduct collapsed.

"*Noooooooo!*" screamed Diesel 10.

Diesel 10 slid over the edge of the viaduct and dropped onto a barge filled with sludge. Off he floated, never to be seen again.

Lily opened her backpack and scooped out the wonderful shavings from the railroad. *"Stoke up the magic in the mountain, and the Lady will smile. . . ."*

"Then watch the swirls that spin so well," Mr. Conductor recited, remembering the rest of the clue to the gold dust.

"So well! A well means water!" shouted Junior.

Lily mixed the shavings with Sodor water and shook them around, as if panning for gold. Then she threw the mixture into the air.

"Gold dust!" everyone yelled.

Back at the magic buffers, Mr. Conductor and Junior recovered their sparkle with the new gold dust. Lily and her grandfather hugged each other with joy.

It was a happy Thomas who puffed home that evening, knowing that a little blue engine like himself had been so very *useful*.